To..

with a heart
full of love

Love is all around Pittsburgh

Copyright © 2016 by Sourcebooks, Inc.
Written by Wendi Silvano
Illustrated by Joanna Czernichowska
Design by Quadrum Solutions (www.quadrumltd.com)

Sourcebooks and the colophon are registered trademarks of Sourcebooks, Inc.
All rights reserved. No part of this book may be reproduced in any form or by any electronic or mechanical means including information storage and retrieval systems—except in the case of brief quotations embodied in critical articles or reviews—without permission in writing from its publisher, Sourcebooks, Inc.

Published by Sourcebooks Jabberwocky, an imprint of Sourcebooks, Inc.
P.O. Box 4410, Naperville, Illinois 60567-4410
(630) 961-3900
Fax: (630) 961-2168
www.sourcebooks.com

Source of Production: Phoenix Color, Hagerstown, Maryland
Date of Production: August 2015
Run Number: 5004410
Printed and bound in the United States of America.
PHC 10 9 8 7 6 5 4 3 2 1

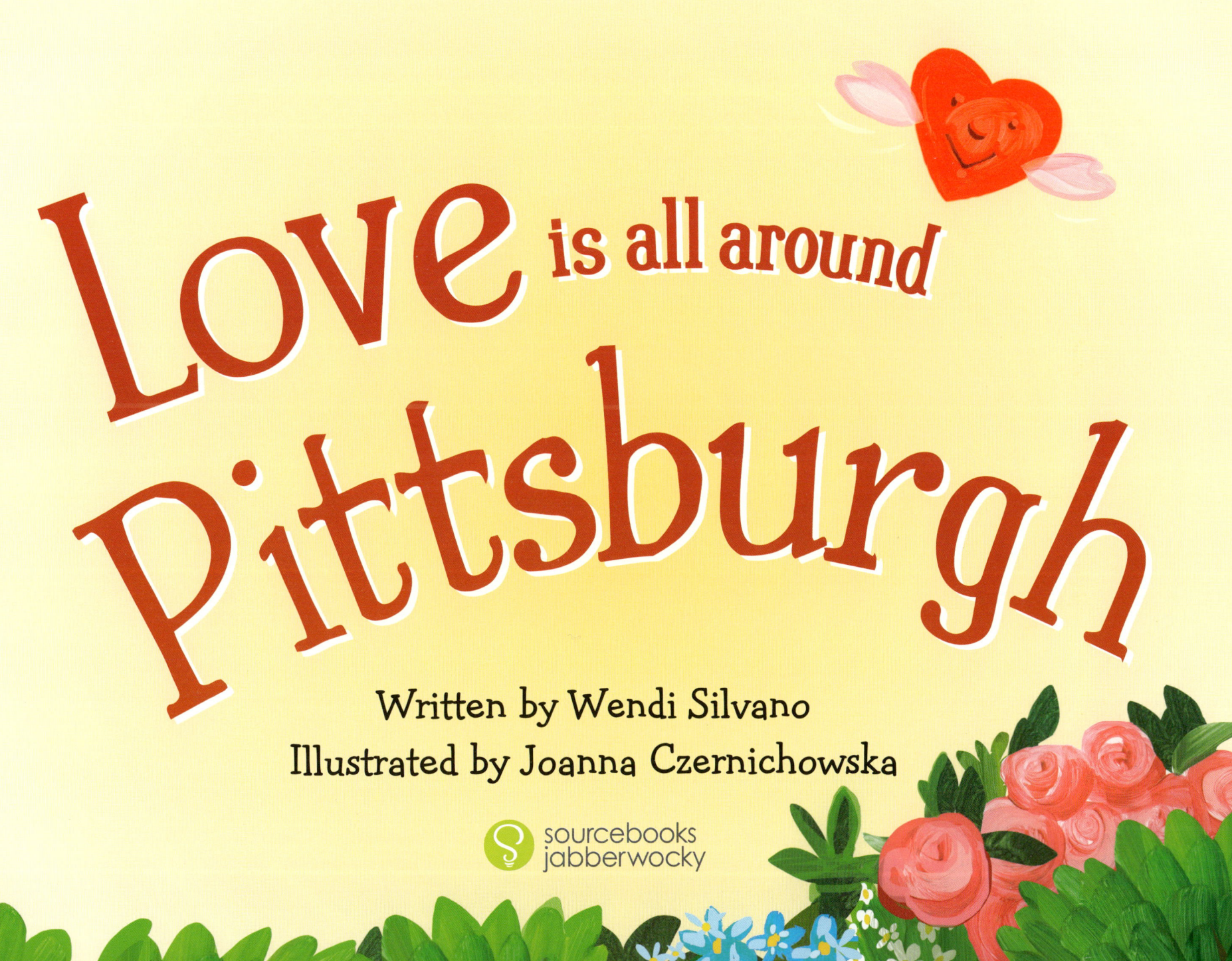

Love is a feeling that comes from **inside**.

Everyone feels it. It can't be denied.

But how do we know that it's there? What's the clue?

How can we **see** it?

Just what can we do?

Love's all around, if you just pay attention,

in people and places too many to mention.

Go look at the **park,**

on the **street,**

at the **mall.**

You'll see love all over. It's **big** and it's small!

All around Pittsburgh, in cars and on trains, in taxis and buses, on boats and on planes, in Regent Square, Hazelwood, and Shadyside too, you'll find there is love that will come into view.

Allegheny River

Right there, on the lawn, in grand Schenley Park is a **mom** with her **babe,** hearing songs of a lark.

She **swaddles** him, **cuddles** him, **kisses** his ear.

That surely is **love**, it's perfectly clear!

At a store in Mount Washington, a girl gets a bear. She **squeezes** him, **squishes** him, **ruffles** his hair.

It's clear that she loves him. She's smiling and bright.
She tucks him in softly and gently at night.

That same little girl, the very next day,
sees a **friend** at her school who is too **sad** to play.

So she sits down beside him and listens and shares, making sure that he knows there's someone who cares.

Now the boy who was **sad** feels much **better**, you see,
so he runs home all happy to play with **Magee**.
They **romp** and they **frolic**.
They **fetch** and they **run**.
It's certain he **loves** him. They're having such **fun**!

You can see how **love** travels
when **shared** with a friend.
If *everyone* shares love, it never will end.
From one to another, it s p r e a d s and it **grows**.
You can't have *too much*, as everyone knows.

A Squirrel Hill officer who **helps** change a flat.

A Highland Park fireman who **rescues** a cat.

HEINZ FIELD

The home team that makes the crowd **cheer** and **clap**.
Each moment has **love** like a **gift** you unwrap.

There's a **father** who sits at the table each night, **helping** out with the homework to get it just **right**. He's tired and busy, but that's **love**, you know... giving up what you want to **help** someone else **grow**.

It's not only *people* who show **love**, it's true.
Just come see the creatures
at the Pittsburgh Zoo!
The polar bear **tumbles**
and **roll**s with her cub,
and when they are finished,
she gives him a **rub**.

Where else is there love? Have we looked all around?

I think we've forgotten—love grows from the ground!

In the meadows and gardens and parks you will find

that the earth shows us love of all shapes and all kinds.

Wherever you look, love comes into sight.

It's there in the morning, it's there in the night.

But all throughout Pittsburgh,

the best love you'll find

is a love that is gentle,

and selfless, and kind…

It's the love found at **home.** It shows up each day
in things people do and in things people say.
There's no greater love, I can tell you, it's true,
than the **love** of your family...

Especially for YOU!